JOYCE CAROL THOMAS

A Mother's Heart,

A Daughter's Love

Poems for us to share

JOANNA COTLER BOOKS

An Imprint of HarperCollins*Publishers*

Acknowledgments

Appreciation everlasting to all gentle and fiercely loving mamas and mothers,

including blood mothers, grandmothers, stepmothers, godmothers, foster mothers,

stand-in mothers, and last but not least, daughters everywhere.

I thank my gracious agent, Anna Ghosh; I thank my editors, Joanna Cotler

and Justin Chanda, for their faithful seeing, again and again.

A special thanks to my daughter, Monica Leona Pecot, for naming this book.

I thank the guiding spirit who has brought us this far.

Library of Congress Cataloging-in-Publication Data
Thomas, Joyce Carol.
  A mother's heart, a daughter's love / by Joyce Carol Thomas
    p.   cm.
  ISBN 0-06-029649-6 — ISBN 0-06-029650-X (lib. bdg.)
  1. Mothers and daughters—Juvenile poetry.   2. Children's poetry, American.   3. Mothers and daughters—
Poetry.   4. American poetry.
PS3570.H565 M68   2001   00-063196
811'.54 21
                Typograph

Central Arkansas Library System
Children's Library
Little Rock, Arkansas

I am all that I am
And some of what I hope to be

For Monica

Contents

Author's Note

IMAGINE THIS: at dawn a river meanders silky as a lullaby, then in the afternoon rushes along a stormy, turbulent course. When evening falls, the river rounds a bend where all is peaceful and calm. I wrote these twenty-five poems of love and longing to reflect that ever-changing waterscape: the lifelong relationship between mothers and daughters.

To make fully apparent the dance between parent and child, these poems are written in two parts—in the voice of a daughter and the voice of a mother. The poems can be read alone or in two parts, out loud. If you choose to read the poems in two parts, the daughter's voice is set in the lines on the left side of each page and the mother's voice is set in the lines on the right side of each page. Like a song, the two parts can be read so that the voices resonate separately, back and forth, in a call and response. When the two voices share the same lines on the page, the voices can be spoken together, as in a duet. As in life, sometimes we stand alone, sometimes there is discord, and sometimes we are in perfect harmony.

What happens when a mother's heart and a daughter's love dip into the river of life? Listen closely to the murmuring echoes as the river curls and rolls through time.

How do we understand that the rhythms of life and love pulsate with laughter, anger, pain, joy, forgiveness? How do we learn to trust the love flowing from heart to

Who Would Come?

Wrapped in a snug blanket
Blinking
New to the light I wait
Not knowing
Who will come
The yearning line unravels

We are a yarn
Of wanting women
Unwinding down
A row of cribs

I am a ball of threads
Crying and crying
A blanket soaked in tears
Inspected, measured
Through my bawling
I hear every wish

Some sigh
"We wanted a boy"
Another whispers
"We're looking for hair
Dark as a raven's wing"
Ignoring me,
The wish line continues
And I curl up
In my ball of security
Then a milky fragrance
Tickles my nose
I sniff like a puppy
Recognizing
The smell
Of its own mother

And I pause
At your cradle

Author's Note

*I*MAGINE THIS: at dawn a river meanders silky as a lullaby, then in the afternoon rushes along a stormy, turbulent course. When evening falls, the river rounds a bend where all is peaceful and calm. I wrote these twenty-five poems of love and longing to reflect that ever-changing waterscape: the lifelong relationship between mothers and daughters.

To make fully apparent the dance between parent and child, these poems are written in two parts—in the voice of a daughter and the voice of a mother. The poems can be read alone or in two parts, out loud. If you choose to read the poems in two parts, the daughter's voice is set in the lines on the left side of each page and the mother's voice is set in the lines on the right side of each page. Like a song, the two parts can be read so that the voices resonate separately, back and forth, in a call and response. When the two voices share the same lines on the page, the voices can be spoken together, as in a duet. As in life, sometimes we stand alone, sometimes there is discord, and sometimes we are in perfect harmony.

What happens when a mother's heart and a daughter's love dip into the river of life? Listen closely to the murmuring echoes as the river curls and rolls through time.

How do we understand that the rhythms of life and love pulsate with laughter, anger, pain, joy, forgiveness? How do we learn to trust the love flowing from heart to heart?

Joyce Carol Thomas

Contents

And rock it
So gently
I pull the thumb
From my mouth
And ask myself
"Who is this?"
You wrap your fingers
Around mine
And whisper in my ear:

Oh, here you are . . .
And then I reach down
And lift you up

You hold me so close
I can hear your heart
Thunder
You hug me as
If you'll never let me go

And I am yours
And you are mine

Through a flood of tears
Drying like water left
Under a summer sun
I can see
That you want me for me
And you want only the best
For me

Cradle

When the sun turns to
Shadow
When I see the moon rise

When I stretch my arms
And yawn
When I rub my sleepy eyes
That's the time
You turn to me
That's the time
You cradle me
Within your arms

When the sky's
A thousand stars

When I hold back
Sleepy sighs

Then you wrap your arms
Around me
And sing sweet lullabies
That's the time you turn
To me

That's the time you
Cradle me
Within your arms

That's the time I
Cradle you
Within my arms

Sugar

Come morning,
You feed me
Mashed wild berries
Sweet

Sweet as the taste of
Your dimples
When I kiss them

And then you coo

Give me some sugar

And you smother
My cheeks
With kisses

Oh those berries
The tangy flavors

I try hard to stay as sweet
As berries in July
But sometimes my mood
Is so sour
It puckers my lips
And you say

I like you just as you are:
Sour or sweet

And you give me that
Mama smile
Patient as summer

Waiting for berries
To ripen   To ripen

The Christening

A twinkle of lights
Flickering from twelve
Candles
The leather smell of the
Good Book
The silver chalice cupping
Water
To bless your innocence

Attendants in swishing
Robes
With so many folds
I cannot count them
Mothers on the front
Bench praying while
Anointed hands sprinkle
Grace
On my hairless head

A bright and shining
Moment

Even though
You are dressed
In your Sunday best
What you're really wearing
Is more than fashion
Can perceive
You're wearing your heart

Like a red ribbon
On my pastel sleeve

No!

Stop that crying
Soap and water
Never hurt a body

Noooo!

Be still while I rinse out
This shampoo
Suds smarting your
Pretty eyes
You're right!
Getting rid of dirt
Can hurt
Be still

No!

Now! Let's open the
Door and go

No!

Don't the plum trees
Look beautiful today?

No!

First Day

I shine your
Kindergarten shoes
And ribbon your braids
And take longer
Than I need
To button the back
Of your blouse

Of my blouse
Early autumn's gaze
Graces my skirt
And does not faze

Or fade
The cotton beauty of
Each pleat, each fold
How did you get to be
Five years old?

Will the teacher like me?
Will I like her or him?
Will I sit next to my
Best friend?
Maybe they won't
Let me in

We'll walk together
I'll sit next to you
Until the bell rings
And then you'll bring   And then I'll bring

Me home   You home

What I Love

What I love about you
Mama, is this:
The smell of your hair
After coconut shampoo
The nape of your neck
Where I nestle my nose
Your fragrant pillow
Your scented clothes

And what I love about you
Sweetie, is this:
Herbal tea steeped in cozy
Morning
Brisk walks up a
Windy hill
Meditation in the silent
Stillness

Delight that laughs away
The chill

Garden weeding

Book reading

Rescuing cats
From the tops of trees

And feeding two birds   And feeding two birds
With one seed   With one seed

Breathing

Your proud smile

Watching you
Breathing notes
In and out of your
Magical fingers
Like air dancing

You are present in my life
At my musical recital
I fumble a passage
You nod encouragement
Only then do I move on
Playing while playing
Giving in to the song
Giving in to the piano
My fingers flying

Effortless across
The now articulate black
And ivory keys

You are present in my life   You are present in my life
To love and adore   To love and adore
To love   To love
To love and adore   To love and adore

                                                   Like a perennial flower

Springing in

                                                   Springing out

Every giving season
Mother mine   Daughter mine
I love you even
More   More

Mother's Day

Dear Mama, I love
The shape of you
Round breasts fluffy
As pillows
Circles with purple grapes
At the center
Your tummy
Sun-streaked peaches
And apricots
Face, a full-moon pumpkin
Soft and firm
Pear-shaped hips
Oval lips
And curved hands
Carrying
A mama basket
Of melons, mulberries,
And mangos

Step!

You danced with me
In your arms
Before I could walk
When I took my first steps

That was then
Now you've got
Long in the legs and arms
In fact, downright gangly

I can outstep you!   I can outstep you!

Moving musicians sizzle
Out of the stereo
You jump so high

You jump so high

                                        Why somebody
                                        Could mistake
                                        You for a note

Dazzling,
High stepping Mama
You cut the rug
And I do too
Every step I take
I got it from you

                                        You step in

And out

                                        Of rhythm

I follow you

Hips swaying   Hips swaying
Eyes dancing   Eyes dancing
Lips firmly pursed

                           Feet swift
My backbone nimble   My backbone nimble

We fly on a river of wood
And we whirl   And we whirl

Up

                           And down the oak floor

'Til the oak boards
Jiggle with joy

Oh, high stepping mama   Oh, high stepping daughter

Step! Step! Step!   Step! Step! Step!

The Game

It's my swiftest game
Springing the ball
Like the globe of the world
It is the world
And I hold the world
In my hand
I bend over and dribble
The world low
All around the court

Go, daughter!
Dance with that ball
You hold the magic
In your mind!
And in your fingers!

Next thing I know
Somebody elbows me

Knocks me flat
On the floor
Mouth smashed in

Your eyes puffed
Your face all purple
Lips bursting like fat plums
Oh no! Time out!
I don't wait for the referee

But it's my game
And I'm ready
To play again
Have to fight my own
Battles
And I still do

How come?
Wonder where
You get that from?

Running Away!

I'm running away
Tired of washing dishes
Making my bed
Raking the lawn
Toasting the bread
For breakfast
I'm running away!

Is that so?
What do you know
That I don't know
Go ahead!
Make a concrete bed!

I shout at you
You shout at me
I pack my bag

Sit on the curb
My frown reads
"Do not disturb"
My appetite smells
Hunger call
You're not thinking about
My wishes
You're in the kitchen
Cooking, stirring up . . .
What's that smell?
Seafood dishes!
My favorite

And we dine

Like somebody
Who chooses Mama
Each day
And chooses not to run
Miles away

So Close

He plants a gardenia

 In the curls of your hair

I take his hands
Rough as redwood

 Stare into his teasing eyes

'Til I hear his heart dancing

His velvet mouth brushes
My eager lips

I taste

 Cinnamon spice

Sprinkled on baked apples Sprinkled on baked apples
Crowned with mulberries
Halo of steam

Up All Night

Mama, Mama, Mama
I want to stay out
All night
I want to dance
'Til dawn's early light
I want to rob today
And save tomorrow
I want to hold my own baby
In my teenage arms
I want to be a woman
Like you, Mom

                              Daughter, Daughter
                              If you have a child
                              Before your time
                              You'll be like a poem
                              Out of rhyme
                              You'll stay up
                              All night, all right

The crying baby
Won't sleep
'Til morning's light
And you won't either
So many ways you'll pay
If you rob tomorrow
And only play today
I love you, Daughter,
With every breath
I breathe
Do the wisdom thing
Play, study, go to college
Make your future sing

Gardening

You show me how
To plant the turnip seeds
Outside the window
While there I feed
Rich and dark
Compost to the flowerbeds
Dusk falls and we witness
Mother Earth in

All her firefly changes
At moonrise, two shooting
Stars zigzag
Across the sky

And we cross our hearts   And we cross our hearts

Whenever there's a change   Whenever there's a change

In the weather
We fall into the habit of
Gardening
You mother the earth

In the weather

Gardening

Just as I mother you

Falling into the habit

Falling into the habit

We rise
In love

We rise
In love

Glances

Mama, why don't you
Like him?
This boy-god, all bronzed
And gold
He moves me 'til my head
Spins and
Art break-dances in
My mind

It's not that I don't like him
It's just that he's from the
Wrong side of life
Wild and disrespectful

You don't understand
You don't like anybody I like
Except the one who gave me
My first kiss

I miss him

But I'm the one who
Kissed him

Forget this new one,
Daughter
Look at him with
Eyes in the back of
Your head

See his backwards spirit

I'll lead him to the right side
The bright side.

It won't work!
No!   No!

When Mama Prays

> "I need thee
> Oh, I need thee
> Every hour . . ."

When Mama prays,
I don't know . . .
I can't tell if she's ecstatic
Or sad
Is she crying for joy?
Or is she crying
To keep from getting mad?
Tears roll down her
Finger-painted cheeks
Like rain used as
God's own brush cleaner
Laughing or crying
Her tears
Mix everything up

In one dizzying moment
I hear
A funeral and
A wedding song playing
Counterpoint
In two far-off places
Mama kneels
By her pew or
By her turned-down bed
Is she calling for help?
Or is she murmuring
To herself?

"I need thee
Oh, I need thee
Every hour I need thee"

Slow, ponderous
Piercing
Why are her prayers
Not luminous?
Like laughter?

Listen, I say, Listen

Graduation

Will Daddy get here
In time?

> Wouldn't miss it
> You know your daddy
> He was ready before me!
> Gone to get some film
> He'll be front row center
> Blinding
> People with the camera

Lights flashing   Lights flashing
Me marching!

> Watching you
> March across
> That stage
> Just look at you!

How I missed that look!
When I was away
I missed you
Like I was missing
A piece of a puzzle
Like I was missing
A part of my mind

I always kept your plate
Waiting at the dinner table
Every time I made
Seafood gumbo
I seasoned the pot
With salty tears
But, Honey, I was
Feeling you
I knew when you needed
To take a
Break and take a nap
In my bones, I knew

Well, if you're feeling me
Now
You know that
Today I feel like
A pretty garden
Sprouting spring leaves

                    Uh-hm
                    Bringing in the sheaves

And making this daughter

                    And making this mama

Light-headed with laughter

                    Happy

Harmony

I keep trying to keep
The promise

           Daughter, you know you are
           My hope!

We dance in harmony's
Silence

           In the rests between notes

Then float out on keys
That syncopate

We tantalize

           We symbolize

We mesmerize

Minds wiggle

Minds wiggle

Bodies giggle

We levitate

We levitate

We percolate

We percolate

Wedding

When you introduced him
To your daddy and me
I liked him so much
I didn't say anything

He was your choice
Afraid that if I spoke my
Mama mind, you might
Not like him as much

I like him so much

Our bodies dance
And shimmer
Like soft rain
On garden stones

Sparkling
Let me see that ring again
The one his mama wore!

The one his mama wore?

A Hope, A Promise

Something in the shadows
Inked in sunlight
Flitting 'cross your face
Tells me
A brand-new child is about
To be born

When my labor gushes
Into water signs
You hold my hand
Watching the show
Of rain
Washing down the hill

Washing down the gift

Washing down the pain

Stop Mothering Me!

Here's a helping of turnips
And black-eyed peas

                    No!
                    Stop mothering me!

Still hot from the stove's
Red eye
And jalapeño cornbread
Steaming from the smoking
Skillet

                    No!
                    Stop mothering me!

How's that flu?
Or are you just plain blue?

                    Stop mothering me . . .

And a brewed cup
Sip it up
Of lemongrass tea

                              I'm unfurling my napkin
                              And getting high
                              Off the smell
                              Of lemon meringue pie

Your meditation on the mix
Of aromas
Works magic on the
Down-turned
Tug of your mouth
Up-righting it into your
Fabulous grin

                              Blues stopped its song
                              And flu soon gone

Paint Me Like I Am

Laughing . . . dancing

Why don't you
Paint me like I am?
Laughing and dancing
And smiling a lot
Running with the children
With the sun in my face
Why don't you
Paint me like I am?

Paint you
Curly-haired and walking
With that amazing grace
Paint you happy
And shouting in the temple

Paint me balancing
Dream baskets of
Passion fruit

On my head

Paint you with the
Elegance
You had when you
Taught me
How to adorn myself and
How to be a woman

Paint me when I remember
That I am the daughter
Of Limpopo legends
Of brooks and streams
And growing green things

Paint you without the tears
And the bowed-down
Expression

Paint me without the ropes

For I am unchained

Can't you hear it

In my voice?

How some wish

They could sing like me

Paint me traveling

Paint me dancing

Paint you free!   Paint me free!

Gone

All of a sudden
It catches my mind
And won't turn loose

Dropping in on me
When I least expect it

In the middle
Of conversations
And courtrooms
And shopping

Ribbons of funeral song
Tie in and out
Of my moments

Echoed organs
Offer
Up the cadence
I cannot moan
I step way back
Inside myself
And look out at the world

How long?
'Til clover stays green
And people die and
Are
Born
Again

Finding You

Mama, I have found you
In the swirl of the wind
In the kaleidoscope
Of the sea
In the mustard covering
The mountains
In the forgiving fields
Of prayer

I have found you
In the indelible places
In the heart of grief
In the soul of sorrow
In my ink pen bleeding
Your laughter and pain

I have found you

Painted in the rainbow
Colors
Of my children
I have found you
Choreographed
In their daring dance

I have found you
Memorable as
Lullaby music
Forever crooning
In my inner ear
An echo ghost
Ever shining
From hallelujah rainbows

Streaking across
Eternity's sky